Sprinkle's Mysterious Collar

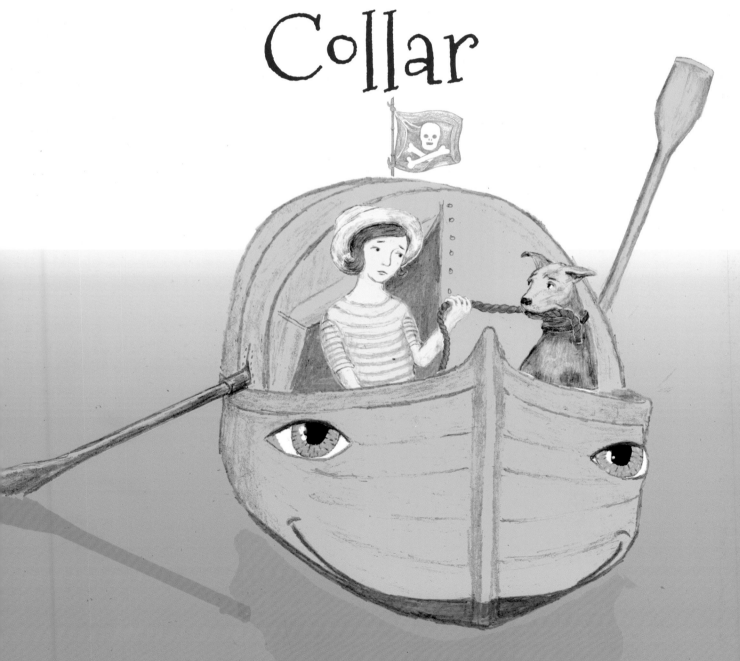

Breakfast

Somewhere in the calm early morning mist along the riverbank ducks were squabbling,

but the little red boat called Flatty dozed on, knowing even in sleep that ducks always fuss over nothing.

The slap of tiny river wavelets,
and the warming sun finally
woke Flatty.

The ducks were now quiet,
too busy with their breakfast to
argue, but the rest of the world
was stirring.

"Morning!" said Flatty, as Lucy came down to the river.
She dipped a bucket in the river and lugged it full and dripping up the path,
and round to the side of The Bokey.

Lifting high, she poured into the hand pump, and started cranking the handle. The pump rattled and croaked a protest as murky river water disappeared down its parched innards. Lucy poured more in and pumped again. Now fresh water surged back up, filtered clean by sand and gravel deep underground. Rinsing and refilling, she now took it round the back to the kitchen, and topped up the old yellow stone water filter standing by the sink.

Flatty could hear Lucy making breakfast - the pop of the primus stove lighting, the rise and fall of the tin whistle on the kettle. The smell of toast and instant coffee drifted across the veranda, where Lucy set the table for breakfast.

"Mind The Gap!" announced Flatty, like a station-master, as Lucy positioned the table and chair legs so to not fall between the floorboards.

"Nothing wrong with a little fresh air to dry out your noggins of a morning," said The Bokey – the wooden bungalow where Lucy spent her summer holidays. It was raised off the ground on brick pillars - just high enough to keep the carpets dry during the winter floods.

Flatty chuckled. The bungalow was a little touchy about the gaps on his veranda. As for Flatty - who was, after all, a rowing boat - a gap of any sort between two planks was unthinkable.

Lucy ignored their banter. What a glorious morning for boiled eggs and soldiers! The sun sparkling on the river, the birds singing!

"Morning Bokey, morning Flatty! Breakfasts Ready!" she called, and then "Come on Sprinkle you old lazybones! Rise and Shine! If I can do it, you can do it!"

A lank sleepy puppy with long wobbly legs and big paws came out and stretched lazily.

Then, seeing the river, it bounded across the grass, down the bank, skidded across the landing stage and fell headlong into the water.

"Good Morning," said Flatty when the dog's head reappeared. "Nothing like a swim before breakfast, is there?"

Gasping and coughing, it doggy-paddled back to shore and tried to climb up, but the landing stage was too high. A hand reached down and, grabbing a handful of floppy puppy skin, hauled him out.

Laughing, Lucy made the introductions: "Flatty this is Sprinkle. Sprinkle this is Flatty." Sprinkle stood there, dripping, with a strange look on his face, then retched and coughed up a small fish - which flapped across the landing stage back into the water.

"Ah that's better!" said Sprinkle, and he shook himself, soaking Lucy and Flatty.
"There's boiled eggs on the veranda," said Lucy smiling. "But I see you have already eaten!"

Old Boatshed

The insides of Old Boatshed smelt of linseed oil, varnish and days gone by.

"Look in the back," called Flatty. "Up on the shelf".

"I see it!" answered Lucy.

She grabbed a bucket, stood on it and climbed up onto a dresser. A huge spider scuttled away.

"Yuck! Horrid Thing! ...Needs a proper cleanout in here, I can tell you!" she said.

"You're telling me," grumbled Old Boatshed.

Lucy examined a wooden rose. One petal was looked different, and... it was loose.

"Found it!" she called and slid a large key out of its hiding place. "Now what?"

"Open the door, back on the right," said Flatty.

"Oi! What's going on?" said Old Boatshed.

The corner was blocked by a stack of dinghies, ropes, oars and cobwebs. Lucy hesitated for a moment. "Get a grip!" she said, and grabbing an odd-looking paddle shaped like a sword, felt much braver. She hacked and poked her way into the corner where a small door was hidden. The key fitted the lock, and the door yielded, but inside was even darker. Lucy shivered and backed out.

"You don't want to go in there," said Old Boatshed.

"We are going to need a torch," she said, pushing hurriedly back and out into the sunlight and warmth of the river bank.

"Are you OK?" asked Flatty.

"Yes, I'm fine," she answered, pulling spider webs off her hair with a shudder.

"Look under my sink," said The Bokey. "Don't mind Old Boatshed. Him and his lot have been sitting there complaining since the Crusades. Miserable and dark, the lot of them!"

"So would you be if you'd been through what we'd seen!" said Old Boatshed crossly. "Stood in the wet hundreds of years - does yer joists in, I can tell you. Just left here to rot in the 'owling sun and the gnashing rain. Never swept out proper, everything dumped in here wot nobody wants, never dusted. Never get me winders cleaned! - Not Never! Got no friends, no family. Me cat died. Did they send another? No nuffink! Eight hundred year I bin looking after The Stuff and never even a thank you. But do I complain? No! Not like some of these 'temporary structures' coming down 'ere nowadays - think they're something special with their poncy pink paint and names like 'Loch Fynn!' and their winders all washed every week. Makes you want to split yer futtocks it does!"

"Now then! Mind your language! There's children present! Load of nonsense, 'howling sun' indeed!" said The Bokey, "'Tis the wind howls, not the sun!" Then changing the subject he said; "Sprinkle, Why don't you go in with Lucy? You might sniff out something interesting."

Lucy found the torch and went back inside Old Boatshed with Sprinkle.

They opened the door again. Inside, a stone tunnel led off into the dark.
Against one wall was and a long box.
Sprinkle trotted off, disappearing into the dark.

"Let's look in the box first!" Lucy called after him, rather more loudly
than she intended.

Old Boatshed's Tunnel

It was just a bit scary in here! The chill air smelt damp and mouldy. The long box looked a little bit like a coffin. Where was that dog? He shouldn't rush off like that!

"Sprinkle!" she called. The sound of her voice echoed down the tunnel as it chased after the dog. A cold chill air returned, as if guarding the entrance against an unwelcome river bank. But she followed – down steps, up steps, round a bend, and down again. Then out into a bell-shaped room, with six sides, each with a tunnel.

"Sprinkle! Where are you?"

Her call echoed around, and died away.

She shone the torch into a tunnel. It seemed too dark, even for the torch.

"I'm not going in there," she said out loud.

"No I wouldn't if I were you," said a familiar voice.

She spun round. "Sprinkle! You naughty dog! Where have you been? I've was really worried about you. Don't ever rush off again like that!" and she sat down suddenly.

Sprinkle bounced up, soaking wet and dripping all over the floor, and licked her.

"Yuck, Get off! You're soaked!"

"You said we were going on an adventure," he said.

"Yes, but not here! We are meant to be going up the river, not crawling around like...like worms in a dungeon and falling in the water. It's not nice in here! Not at all what one ought to find in a properly run boatshed!"

"Look, what I found," said Sprinkle, holding out a dog collar.

It was formed of fine strands of black wire, woven together to resemble snakes twisting around and swallowing their tails. Every inch or so around the collar was studded with a dark jewel.

"Wow!" said Lucy. "This is treasure! It's beautiful. Let me put it on you!"
As Lucy buckled the collar around Sprinkle's neck, it began to glow. The woven band of black wires shone the colour of gold, and the studs glowed green.
"What's happening?" said Sprinkle, feeling light headed, which indeed he was.
"It lit up," said Lucy. "Look!" and she turned the torch off.

The walls of the chamber shimmered gold and green, and as Sprinkle turned his head the patterns of light moved with him.
"It feels funny" he said. "I can smell better. Every smell seems so clear and sharp. It is almost painful. Hmm, most interesting!" and he started sniffing around the floor and wagging his tail.

"I don't like the sound of that!" said Lucy, "I remember a story where that sort of thing happened and it just caused a load of trouble. You better take it off," and she turned the torch on again.

As the collar came off, the lights went out, and the collar became black again.

"You don't want to believe everything you read in stories," said Sprinkle.

"Dog collars don't just light up in the dark in real life," said Lucy.

"What about the one I got for Christmas?" said Sprinkle.

"But that had a battery in it," said Lucy; "This is different. This might be magic."

"So?"

"So, it might not be nice. I don't know. It might take control of you, or something nasty might happen....There was this doctor who sold his soul to the devil so he could know everything."

"Well, - I'm going not going to be a doctor, I'm going to be a soldier, and anyway, I belong to you so I can't sell myself, can I?"

"That's right. You're just a puppy. So don't run off like that. I was worried!"

"Okey Bokey!"

"What?"

"Okey Dokey! Won't run off... Well, try not to,... except when it's exciting...perhaps," said Sprinkle.

"Let's go back and get the camping equipment. Flatty said it's just inside the door in the long box," said Lucy.

"Can I wear the collar?"

"Yes, on one condition, and that is :- if you feel like taking over the world, or being the most powerful dog in the universe, or selling your eternal soul to the devil, or any other weird stuff happens - you must take it off immediately, OK?"

"OK..... Is it OK if it lights up?" he asked

"Yes I suppose so."

"And is it OK if I can smell better?"

"No!!"

"Ow-oh. Please?"

"No!"

"But what's wrong with that? It's no different than someone wearing glasses."

"It's not natural!"

"Spoil sport!"

"Stop it Sprinkle! I'm the Mummy and I know what's best! I don't want to hear any more about it. Now let's go back,..... Er, which way was it?"

"Don't know!" said Sprinkle sulking.

"Right! We are going this way!" said Lucy, and she marched into a tunnel.

But it was the wrong tunnel and they came out into another, identical, bell-shaped room with six tunnels leading from it.

She said "Help me!"

"Can I wear it?" he said.
"No... I mean...
Oh well - you wretched dog!
Yes, just this once!"
She fastened Sprinkle's collar back
on, he sniffed the air once, and led
them straight back to the entrance.

Back in the boatshed he was almost overpowered by impressions from the sleepy musky damp river, the pungent boat varnish, the creosote, pitch, paint and rope. Smells of ancient China threaded down through the rafters.

Then back outside in the bright sun to a blizzard of smells - so sharp and crisp that they pricked at his mind like a cheese grater. Rich sickly hues sent him hot and cold. He must not throw up now, or Lucy would know and take the collar away!

"You've been a long time," said Flatty.

"Look what I found!" he said at last, showing his collar. It had turned black in the sunlight.

"Oh! That old thing. I've not seen it for years!" said Flatty.

"Is that dog nicking My Stuff?" asked Old Boatshed.

"Is it safe?" asked Lucy.

"I wouldn't worry," said Flatty "It glows sometimes. Sprinkle is just borrowing it. Are you feeling OK?" Sprinkle nodded, his eyes watering.

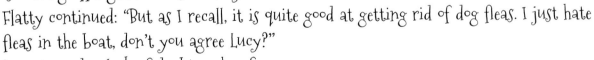

"Good!" continued Flatty "You might get a slight headache – nothing to worry about."

"Headache? What headache? What do you mean? ...That collar is coming off right now!" said Lucy.

Flatty continued: "But as I recall, it is quite good at getting rid of dog fleas. I just hate fleas in the boat, don't you agree Lucy?"

Lucy paused, a look of doubt on her face.

Flatty continued:" ... And it gets rid of blood-sucking ticks – which carry all those dreadful diseases. They don't bother me of course – but don't worry, Lucy, you can burn them off your skin with a cigarette..."

At this both Lucy and Sprinkles' eyes widened.

Flatty went on; "And don't worry, Old Boatshed, nobody is going to nick your stuff! Sprinkle is just borrowing it, aren't you Sprinkle? Besides it's meant to be used. That's what you want isn't it?"

"S'pose so," grumbled Old Boatshed; "As long as he brings it back. That's valuable, that is!"

"But what about the camping gear?" asked Flatty.

What to take?

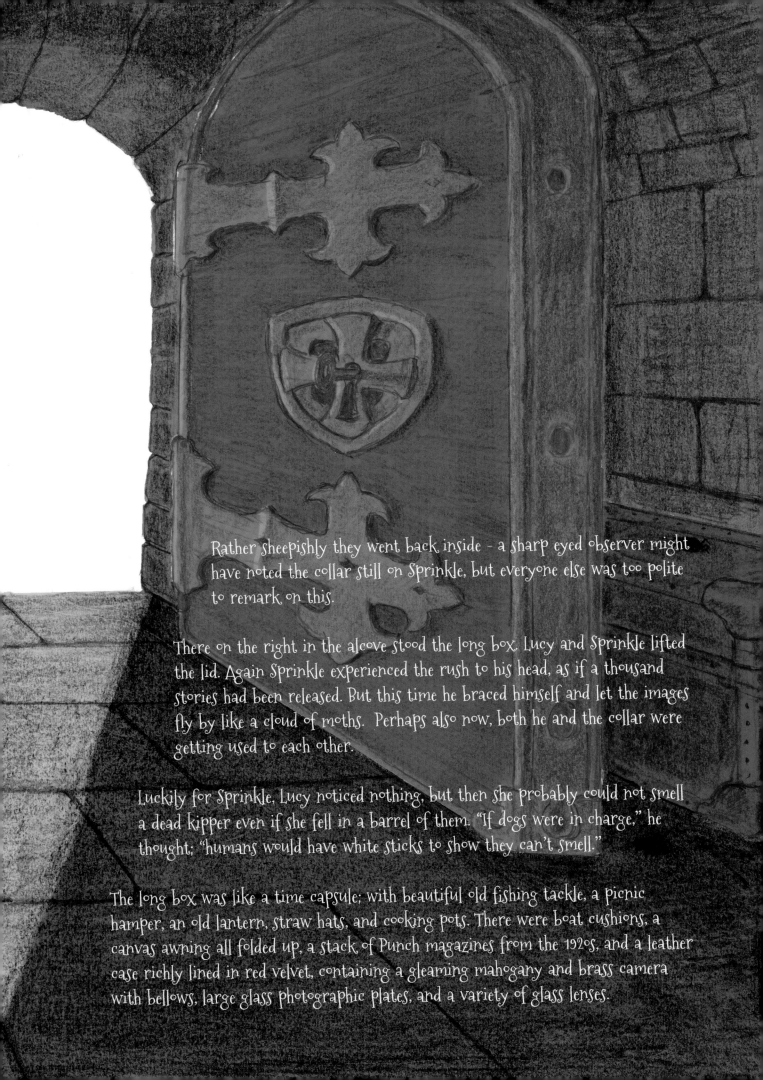

Rather sheepishly they went back inside - a sharp eyed observer might
have noted the collar still on Sprinkle, but everyone else was too polite
to remark on this.

There on the right in the alcove stood the long box. Lucy and Sprinkle lifted
the lid. Again Sprinkle experienced the rush to his head, as if a thousand
stories had been released. But this time he braced himself and let the images
fly by like a cloud of moths. Perhaps also now, both he and the collar were
getting used to each other.

Luckily for Sprinkle, Lucy noticed nothing, but then she probably could not smell
a dead kipper even if she fell in a barrel of them. "If dogs were in charge," he
thought, "humans would have white sticks to show they can't smell."

The long box was like a time capsule; with beautiful old fishing tackle, a picnic
hamper, an old lantern, straw hats, and cooking pots. There were boat cushions, a
canvas awning all folded up, a stack of Punch magazines from the 1920s, and a leather
case richly lined in red velvet, containing a gleaming mahogany and brass camera
with bellows, large glass photographic plates, and a variety of glass lenses.

They dragged most things out, through the boat house into the bright sunshine, and spread it out on the grass.

"Now this is what I call a proper expedition," said The Bokey.

"It's outrageous!" said Old Boatshed. "Bring it back! I'm not...I'm not ready... You haven't got a proper requisition. It's too much! ....Oh no.. not the teapot!"

"Stop it! Get a grip man! You're embarrassing us!" said The Bokey, and everybody else pretended not to notice.

"Let's get your covers on," Lucy said to Flatty. "Do you remember how it goes?"
"Do I remember?" laughed Flatty "Of course I do. Let's put the metal hoops in. It helps to wax 'em first shipmates!"

Along Flatty's sides were a row of holes to fit the hoops in. Lucy rubbed the ends with an old candle, and they slid easily into the sockets.

Next they gave the canvas a good brushing and then a scrub with soap and water on the grass, to clean off the cobwebs, and left it to dry. With the sun shining this didn't take long, and soon they were fitting the canvas over Flatty's hoops. All along the sides they tied down the flaps with cords and tapes, until there was just one flap left open. Inside was warm and cosy like a tent. The light was green, flecked with sunlight reflecting off the water.

"Oh it's lovely in here!" said Lucy. "Let's sleep here tonight! What fun it will be!"

Lucy and Sprinkle spent the rest of the afternoon cleaning the equipment, putting it in Flatty, rearranging it, taking it out again, and discussing the best place for everything.
They made lists of food and equipment needed for the journey. They nipped out to the shops more than once for things they had forgotten, and argued over what to take and what to leave behind.

"I want my paints," said Sprinkle; "my bone, my new collar, this old box camera, the fishing gear and the coffee pot."

"And I want to take my books, swimming togs, the baking tin, all the hump-dumplings and the guitar," said Lucy.

Sprinkle sighed. The hump-dumplings were disgusting old rag dolls with faces, arms and legs but no bodies. Such sissy girly stuff! What a way to run an expedition!

And anyway, all this gear just would not fit, or Flatty would say he felt too full, and so they'd take it all out again and start again, arguing all the while.
Finally they agreed, more or less on what to take, and nobody wanted to spend anymore time talking about it. The Bokey said they should not take the camera, as it was too valuable. Lucy resolved to smuggle her three favourite hump-dumplings aboard by stuffing them in her knickers, and Sprinkle quietly hid his best bone in his blanket.

The boat was quite full, but not too full. It was quite heavy, but not too heavy, and anyway, Flatty would be doing most of the rowing and he was very strong.

Nobody mentioned the odd paddle shaped like a sword. It found its way into the boat, and seemed to belong there. Had they discussed it, I expect Lucy would have said that you always need a spare paddle, and Sprinkle would have agreed, thinking it might come in useful for fighting off pirates, over the head, Thwack! – like that!

Then Aunty Dolly made an official inspection of the ship's provisions, which consisted of two tins each of spam, sardines and baked beans, a bag of liquorice allsorts, half a packet of jammy dodgers and a bottle of lemonade. "This will never do," she said, and went back into the kitchen, from which she later emerged with a rich fruit cake, a huge stash of sandwiches, a large pot of brown Windsor soup, and a milk churn for drinking water.

Just before they left, Police Boat Fred came by.
"Officer! They are nicking My Stuff!" called out Old Boatshed suddenly.

"Don't mind him, Constable," said The Bokey. "He's so old he's forgotten why he's looking after it. I said they could borrow it. They'll be fine."

"Going up river, you say?" said Fred. "Thought I might have a quick word with Flatty, before you go,...that is - private like."

Lucy and Sprinkle sniffed, but they took the hint, got out and went into the bungalow. Then Fred said to Flatty "There's been reports of some funny stuff been going on up river. Could be smuggling – drugs, guns and such-like. Don't know for sure. Anyroad, keep your eyes peeled matey."

"Of course, officer...what fun!" said Flatty.
And stay out of trouble. Don't be a hero, just give me a call if you see anything."
"Right-oh" said Flatty, "I will call you when we get back. See you in a few weeks."

Up River

Lucy and Flatty knew about locks – the boating kind.
After all, they had once been all the way down the
Thames and back again, looking for The Plug Hole.
But Sprinkle had not grown up on the river,
 messing about in boats, and he *kept* falling in!
Lucy decided he fell in on purpose.
"That dog is turning into a show-off," she thought.
The first lock was Penton Hook.
"How are you today Penton?" called Flatty.

Mustn't Grumble. Apart from me hinges is playing up chronic like, of cours't.
Don't make 'em like they used to, Flatty. An' the engineers! Don't talk to me about they!
Kids outa' school nowadays. It's the government to blame, and them in fancy suites wot
come down 'ere! Call 'emselves the Thames Conservancy!   Huh! Couldn't conserve a pot of
jam between the lot o' they... See you got company. Where's you orf to then?"
"Up river. It's a sort of expedition to have adventures. Perhaps we may find The Source!"
 "Tell 'im something from me, will you? Say Penton says stop pouring them vile chemicals in.
 Tainted it is! Causing all the poor little fishes to suffer".

"It's not right I keep telling 'em but they don't listen!
Tell 'im if 'e don't stop we're all going on strike
if we don't all die first. I've done it before.
You tell him. I got my powers I have. You may
laugh – tell him – but he ain't seen nuffink.
Us locks an' weirs can stop the whole river!
So don't go messing – that's what I says-
You tell 'im!"

DEAD SLOW

FLATTY

"Right ho Penton! By the way this is Sprinkle.
It's his first time. Go easy on him or you'll have
him in the drink."

"Don't want no dawgs in 'ere anyroad.
Bad enough with all these plastic gin palaces falling apart!
Don't make boats proper no more.
You should see what ends up in 'ere.
Trash it is, all nasty plastic bits.
Not Safe it h'aint. Stay in the boat 'swot I say.
Helf an' Safety, helf an' safety! Do they listen? No.
Nah in the old days you'd get proper wood, nice mahogany,
teak, proper rope fenders.
Floated in – floated out – no trouble.
Now it all ends up in 'ere all tangled up like a great lump.
How the mighty 'ave fallen. That's wot I say.
Nah stop interrupting me, cos' I got more customers,
and don't fall in."
The lock was filling up with large snooty plastic motor boats.

"They have no idea" said Flatty. "You'd think they were motor cars, all they know is rushing about. Their idea of a pleasant Sunday afternoon is to race from one lock to the next."
Lucy and Sprinkle didn't like them much either, they preferred the quieter boats. Sprinkle liked canal boats, Lucy liked canoes, and Flatty's favourite was clearly sailing boats. Penton shut the gates whilst delivering a stern lecture to all on the importance of saving water. They were in a deep pit dripping with green slimy moss and water weed. Then the sluice gates opened and, with a roar, water rushed in. The boats were jostled about as the lock started to flood. Sprinkle looked around in alarm. Once he realised they would not sink he relaxed, but barked rude remarks at any boat that bumped them.
The water quietened down and they rose serenely to the top. The upstream gates opened and one by one, with much grumbling and bumping, the large noisy motor boats left, each receiving a stern lecture on minding your wash, river bank erosion, speed limits, waste disposal, and much else besides.

Then it was Flatty's turn. He landed a little way upstream and Lucy and Sprinkle walked back to the lock keeper's cottage to buy ice creams, round the side at the kitchen door. Back on the bank they sat down to watch the river and eat their ices. A pretty little sailing boat with the name "Simone" come through the lock, her teak and mahogany decks picked out with bright brass fittings glinting in the sunshine. From her stern a small French flag flew. Her sails and mast were lowered, Flatty said, because there were so many bridges. She chugged past gently, hardly making any wash, and smiled at Flatty. "Ah - the smell of real French coffee!" he said smiling back. They watched her go round the bend. "When you two are older I'd like to do that trip again."
"Where?" said Lucy.
"To France – up the Seine to Paris, the French canals, baguettes for breakfast – rows of beautiful tall poplar trees along the banks, the sun, wine – good French companions - that was the life!"

Simone in trouble

They met Simone again just past Staines.

"Bonjour, Hello again," she called to Flatty with another smile.

"Bonjour, Simone, - Are you OK?" called Flatty.

"Oh Poof! I am a leetle tired. I have no strength today! I just can't move! I think it was that long trip yesterday."

"Let me take a look" he said coming alongside. "Aha! I see. No wonder, you have a rope wrapped round your propeller shaft!"

"Then I am stuck!" she said.

"Don't worry!" said Flatty "We can help. Let me introduce Lucy and Sprinkle!"

"Pleased to meet you," said Lucy .

"Hello!" said Sprinkle.

"Sprinkle is a great swimmer," said Flatty. "He'll have you free in no time. Just keep still and rest up a bit, while we get organised."

"Please be careful," she said.

"Now Sprinkle," whispered Flatty "Dive under Simone and pull the rope off. While you are down there, sniff around a bit - check for anything unusual but don't say anything about it, OK?"

"OK my Capitain," said Sprinkle, and he leapt overboard, landing with a great bellyflop splash and tried to dive down, but came up coughing.

"You forgot the collar!" said Flatty.

"Here you go," said Lucy, and reaching down she put it on. Sprinkle dived down again. This time it was easier and he did not run out of breath. The collar lit up the underside of the boat. There was the propeller with a rope, well and truly wrapped around it. He bit hold of the rope and pulled. He pulled harder. He growled and shook the rope. He put all his paws against the underside of the boat and heaved. "Rooah! GGGRRGGHH. Take That and THAT!!"

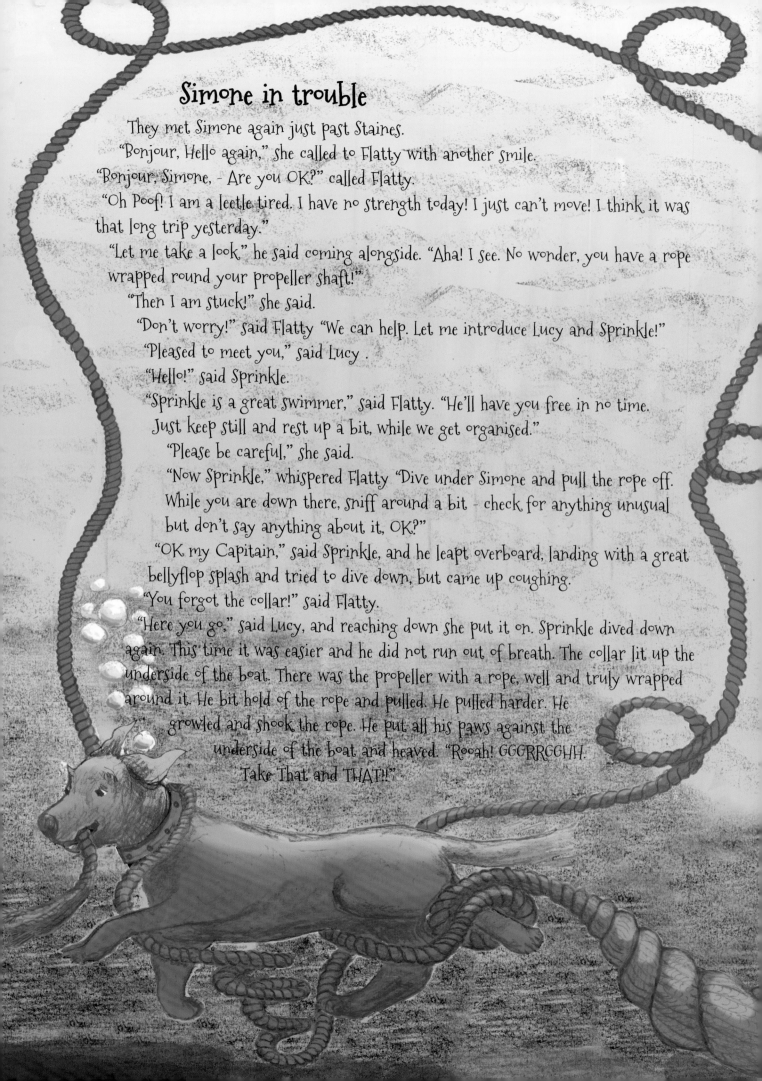

It was coming!!. "Fight it Grrr... Pull and PULL! and shake that nasty ropy thing."
."OW, ow OW!" called Simone.
"Stop it! Sprinkle!" called Lucy.

But Sprinkle was too excited to hear. The rope is a serpent thrashing back and forth. Pull it back! Jerk and snatch, back and back, turning and twisting. It is weakening – he is winning! Suddenly he feels the gravel of the river bed under his feet. He fights in the shallows. Spray flies everywhere. Roaring defiance at the huge killer snaky rope monster, barking and growling with his jaws clamped shut, then up on the bank, back and forth, like a lunatic!

Crash! He falls back in the water. Everything goes quiet. The rope stopped fighting. Sprinkle rose back up to the surface, waving the rope about and sneezing.

"He's done it! Harrah!" called Lucy.

"Oh thank you Sprinkle!" said Simone.

"Try the engine," said Flatty.

Simone started her motor, revved it a few times, put it in gear, drove forwards, drove backwards, stopped again, announced it had never been better, said how sorry she was that she couldn't stop, but perhaps they would meet up at Windsor, and carried on up river. They all watched her go round the bend.

"Well, see anything?" asked Flatty.

"I forgot," said Sprinkle, a little ashamed; "that rope ...."

"...You're completely out of control. Do you know that?" said Lucy crossly; "And anyway, see what? What were you two whispering about? And while we are on the subject, what was all that with Police Boat Fred?"

"You are right," said Flatty "So let me tell you. Fred thinks smugglers might be operating on the Thames, and asked me to keep a look out."

"Smugglers!" said Lucy and Sprinkle.

"What? -You think Simone is mixed up in it?" asked Lucy. "I thought you fancied her! All that smiling stuff. Smell the coffee? When all along you were thinking to yourself 'ah, a nasty sneaky Frenchy criminal. I'll set my spies onto her' - and smile like a two-faced double-dealing ....How could you?"

"I just asked Sprinkle to look around," said Flatty.

"But you smiled!" said Lucy

"So!... she smiled," said Flatty. "What would you have me do? She may be genuine, she may not. We don't know. Don't get upset about it. We hardly know her."

"I don't like this," said Lucy frowning. "You ought to trust people, and be nice to them."

"We were nice. We helped her, remember?"

"The keel smelt funny!" said Sprinkle suddenly.

"I thought you said you forgot to look," said Lucy.

"I did forget. It just came to me."

"So, she could have just run aground on some smelly mud or something," said Lucy; "Anyway, you can't smell underwater. You were just imagining it, just like you imagined you were fighting a monster!"

"You did get carried away a bit," said Flatty. "But there again, you had the old collar on. Did it smell bad before or after the monster raving loony rope bit occurred?"

"Before," said Sprinkle.

"What sort of bad smell...like rotten eggs, burnt toast, dead bodies...what?" asked Flatty.

"Cold. It smelt cold...and black."

"That's not a smell. You can't smell cold or black," said Lucy scornfully; "anyway that doesn't make her a smuggler."

"The truth is - we don't know," said Flatty. "She did leave rather abruptly and didn't invite us to see her again at Windsor, but she does have a rather pretty clinker bottom..."

"Oh how rude!" said Lucy.

"What's she on about?" asked Sprinkle.

"Time to pitch camp for the night" said Flatty. "After supper I might tell you a story about this place. It is called Runnymede."

"What sort of story?" asked Lucy "Real or pretend?"

"Real," said Flatty. "A long time ago, on this spot, the rebel barons forced the King to meet their demands. I was there." [1]

"Cool! Was anyone killed?" asked Sprinkle.

"Sprinkle!" said Lucy "How many times do I have to tell you? Fighting is wrong!"

"I only asked. What *is* your problem!?" said Sprinkle.

"Now now!" said Flatty.

---

[1] **Flatty and the Magna Carta**

Brown Windsor Soup

"Faw! It's disgusting., I never want to see another drop! Even just thinking about it makes me feel sick!" said Sprinkle.

"But it's good for you!" said Lucy.

"S'horrid horrid horrid horrid Yaowoooooh....
Yaowooooh.Ya Ya Yaow! Yaowooh" howled Sprinkle.

"That's a 'no' then," said Flatty.

"Ee does not like your Aunty Dolly's cookeeng," said Simone. "Purr-aps she 'as too much vinaigre?"

"It's that horrid old dog collar!" said Lucy. "He get's picky about his food every time he puts it on."

"A dog's gotta do what a dog's gotta do!" said Sprinkle.

"And you watch too much television," she added.

"What have you gotta' do Sprinkle?" asked Flatty.

"I'm a going in them thar hills and I'm agoin' to find me some real chow. Might kill a moose ah might," announced Sprinkle.

"You could try the butcher's shop up by the Castle," said Flatty.

"Can you get some milk?" called Lucy.

"Pah! Pussy stuff" spat Sprinkle; "Real dogs drink raw blood."

"OK! We get the general idea," said Flatty. "A good run should calm you down. Back on board by ten OK?"

"Wuff!" came the reply as Sprinkle bounded away.

"That dog!" said Lucy.

You worry about 'is collar. Is that she is too tight Lucy?" asked Simone.

"Er..no..It's just a bit weird. Sprinkle thinks it helps his sense of smell."

"I could do with a good sniffere dog," said Simone.

"Why's that?" said Lucy.

"I work for the French Customs Police. In my job a good dog is very 'elpful."

"Are you following someone?" said Flatty.

"That big one moored at the pub, see it? I 'ave followed 'eet from Paris.

"We don't actually know anything about the collar," said Lucy. "Sprinkle says it helps, but for all I know it's just his fertile doggy imagination working overtime."

"Mind you, there may be something in it," said Flatty.

"Why you think is special, this collear?" said Simone.

"Oh...it's very old. ...has been lying around in the boathouse donkeys years," said Flatty.

"Lights up in the dark, but only on dogs. Quite interesting really."

"Oh I know!" said Simone "My dog at 'ome 'as one, but she won't wear eet - says it makes 'er look stupide like the Christmas tree. I tell 'er she must or she can't go out at night – the roads in Paris – you know – ees so dangereus!"

At that point they were interrupted by a couple walking along the bank.

Hello! It's Flatty isn't it?" said the lady. "How are you?"
"Very well ma'am," said Flatty, "I did not recognise you."
"Good! That was the idea. But now you have, let me introduce
my friend Charles, from France. Charles this is Flatty,
our local floating cosmic phenomenon."

"Bonjour Monsieur," said Flatty in his best French, adding "More comic than cosmic I should say – and that's on a good day."

The Frenchman smiled back: "I too have an eye for the ..ah..aqueous humeur. For sure we will be friends. please introduce me to these charming ladies."

"Of course." said Flatty "This is Lucy, from Laleham and Simone – from La Rochelle".

"Enchanté," said Charles nodding; "I ham very pleased to meet you."

"Ow did you know where I come from Flattee?" said Simone.

"I have made a particular study of boat bottoms," said Flatty with a chuckle.

"Oh you men!" said Simone indignantly.

"Good morning Madame. Good morning Monsieur Le President," said Simone.

"What?" said Lucy.

"Eet seems zat Flattee 'as friends in 'igh places," said Simone.

"Oh Lord!" said Lucy going pink" You're not...."

"'Fraid so, but it's our morning orf. Dressed in our cognitos!" said the Queen. "So Mums the word! Ha Ha! I just love messing about in boats, don't you Charles?"

"Verree interressont ma'am - particularly the sailing."

"Would you like to come for a row?" asked Lucy.

"Rather!" said the Queen "....Oh Bother! I've a whole coach load of ancient Knights of the Garter due in at twelve. They get so cross when they have to wait for their dinner."

"How about tomorrow?" said Lucy.

"Yes! I'll bring a picnic," said the Queen; "cucumber sandwiches...and some lovely brown Windsor soup in a thermos!"

Flatty appeared to choke - a quite remarkable sound for a boat, and Lucy looked alarmed.

"..........I have some good French wine" Simone eventually volunteered.

"Beats soup any day," said the President with relief.

"Wait till you try mine!" said the Queen.

"That's a date then," said Flatty.

"Sadly, pressing and urgent affairs of state call me away tomorrow," said the President recovering "You know how it is. But I am very glad to have met you Flatty and Lucy - if you are ever in France, please come and visit. I will show you my fine telescope."

The couple took their leave and Flatty, Lucy and Simone watched as they walked away, discretely shadowed by their minders – until finally they all disappeared around a corner. Then they all broke out in laughter.

"You should have said!" said Lucy.

"No, he's your dog. You should have said!" said Flatty.

"Poor Sprinkle 'e will 'ave to drink eet!" said Simone.

"And the President!" said Flatty "Did you see his face?"

"It's so unfair! I'm glad I'm not the Queen," said Lucy.

"I'm glad I'm not Sprinkle!" said Simone, "Are you going to tell 'im?"

A right royal picnic

All though the night rain drummed on the old green canvas boat cover. Inside Lucy and Sprinkle felt snug and safe, one in salmon pink jimjams and sleeping bag, and the other on a favourite stinky old blanket with a slight lump in it.

Imagine lying in bed, under the green canvas, making your breakfast without having to get up. What bliss! Yet at the same time it is an extremely dangerous operation without the right kit, so don't attempt this at home. Apart from the merely life-threatening dangers of fire and spilt, boiling water, there is the altogether more serious matter of crumbs and jam in the bedding – unless you are a dog, of course. But for humans there is no cure known to science apart from a traumatic trip to a washing machine, or some other equally invasive procedure involving soap and water.

So next morning, in an altogether darker frame of mind, prompted by these risks no doubt, as well as the odd crack of thunder, Lucy contemplated the coming picnic. Just her luck - her only chance to have tea with the... you know who, even on an off day.

Sprinkle, on the other hand, was as happy as ever. Being fast asleep may have had something to do with it, or maybe he was just pretending and actually thanking his lucky stars he didn't have to drink any...well, you know what, and particularly not on an off day.

There was one amongst this happy band who shared, with ducks, no qualms about a picnic in the rain. So without disturbing the occupants, Flatty caste off and sculled quietly up river past the water meadow, and into Windsor, where he hove-to just off the steps by the castle water-gate.

In its day this had been a main entrance to the castle, but now, through years of neglect - or careful attention to detail - not many people were aware of it.

A figure appeared in a doorway as Flatty drew alongside.

Lucy poked her head out of the canvas. "Oh Golly!" she said and dived back inside.
"Hello, Flatty! I'll open up. Just go round," said the Queen and she too disappeared.

The old historic water gate eventually opened after much grumbling. Flatty entered with a polite "Good morning" into a dim tunnel. The gate wheezed shut again, blocking off light and sound from the river. Luckily Sprinkle's collar started to glow.

The Queen reappeared on a small jetty and Flatty drew alongside.

Lucy, now dressed, helped the Queen step across onto Flatty.

"Welcome aboard again," said Flatty.

"Sorry about the gate," she said; "My! This is cosy. Goodness - a luminous dog!"

"This is Sprinkle," said Lucy; "Sprinkle this is the Queen...Sprinkle talks you know! Say hello nicely."

"Hello nicely," said Sprinkle.

"I am very pleased and enlightened to meet you Sprinkle," said the Queen. "Now about this picnic. It's too horrid out. I'd invite you up to the castle for tea, but then Flatty would be left out – and we need to have a little talk. So next best thing, actually a rather royal brainwave – Let's picnic in the old boathouse!"

"Underground?" asked Sprinkle.

"Ah, wait and see! Full speed ahead on engines!" said the Queen.

Flatty set off along the curving tunnel, lit by Sprinkle standing in the bows.

It was quite a long way, thought Sprinkle. They must be going right under the town. He sniffed the air and imagined the faintest echoes of times long past, of grim soldiers and the rattle of armour, boats laden with spices, wine and gold, tradesmen calling, actors in masks, children laughing, voices arguing, a fire, houses burning, a woman calling for help.

"I'm coming!" called Sprinkle.

"What?" said Flatty.

"The lady!" said Sprinkle, as if waking – and puzzled.

"She's in trouble! We must help her."

"There is no one here except us," said Flatty.

"What did she look like?" said the Queen.

"Green dress, red hair, a gold broach – I smelt burning!"

How remarkable!" said the Queen. "Tell me, Sprinkle, what sort of broach was it?"

"A red stone, with gold leaves -like on a scout badge, Didn't you see?"

"We saw nothing Sprinkle. Perhaps you imagined it," said Flatty quietly.

"Wow!" said Sprinkle sitting down.

"Are you OK?" asked Lucy.

"It's that collar isn't it Flatty?" said Sprinkle.

But Flatty said nothing. They had reached the end of the tunnel. It was blocked by another large gate.

"I say there! Open up!" called the Queen, but nothing happened.

"Give it a shove Flatty, if you don't mind. Must be asleep. This whole tunnel gives me the heebie jeebies. Was a time One would have had a gate orf his hinges for less than this - and his head with it, if he'd had one! Ah, those were the days! Now One's Royal Command Performance is more likely to be mistaken for a slightly dodgy variety show up the West End...And you know what? They never asked me to perform, not even once! And I *do* do a nifty Shuffle Back to Baltimore..... 'Five foot two, eyes of blue'...Whoops! ..   Sorry!"

Flatty shoved on the gate...and it opened. They were through, out in to the light on a small calm lake, grey in the steady drizzle, surrounded by gardens and heavy wet willow trees. The Queen directed Flatty to a boathouse at the far end.

"Where are we?" asked Lucy.

"We've gorn round the back," said the Queen, "Look!" and there up the misty hillside they saw the castle.

"Not bad!" said Sprinkle, his spirits reviving in the fresh air.

Did the Knights enjoy their lunch?" asked Lucy.

"Rather!" said the Queen. "Clean wiped me out of soup!"

Sprinkle brightened considerably.

"I had to make some more!" she said.

Sprinkle slumped.

"But guess what?
It got burnt and I had to threw it away," she continued.

Sprinkles eyes widened.

"What a shame!" said Lucy.

Sprinkle did a creditable imitation of sad.

"So it's just cheese and ham sandwiches!" said the Queen.

"Ah!" said Sprinkle and Lucy together.

"Sorry," said the Queen.

"No, no!" said Sprinkle "Not to worry. We like sandwiches - don't we Lucy?"

"You are just saying that. People are always doing that, to butter me up."

"Well, actually, I was thinking about the brown Windsor soup," said Sprinkle.

"Yes of course you were, poor Sprinkle!" said the Queen sympathetically. "But never mind. Stiff upper lip and all that eh?"

"Sprinkle!" said Lucy "Stop it! I'm glad I'm not the Queen. It must be horrid."

And now the Queen was puzzled, but she was not head of the Commonwealth for nothing, and so let it rest.

"About the tunnel..." she said to Sprinkle.

"Spooked me!" he said.

"They do say it is haunted." said the Queen.

"Why did you ask about the broach?" he asked.

"She always wears it," said the Queen. "I have one just like it."

"And who is *she*?" said Lucy.

"There is a story that King Charles gave it to his mistress. She had many enemies of course. During the Great Fire of London she was kidnapped, brought here and drowned. Just a story of course, but one must do one's bit for the great British tourist industry, don't you agree Sprinkle?"

"Yes Ma'am. But if you don't mind my saying - I can't tell when you're pulling my legs," said Sprinkle.

"Oh excellent!" said the Queen chuckling.

The Queen gives Flatty a right royal talking to

The rain stopped and Lucy and Sprinkle went for an explore round the castle grounds, so the Queen could have her "little talk".

"Look, Flatty, you must help us on this climate change thingy" said the Queen.

"What can I do?" said Flatty.

"There must be something!" she said.

"Why do you say that? After all, it's man-made, so you fix it" he said.

"I'm doing my bit. What about you?"

"Even if I wanted to help, do you really think a wooden rowing boat is going to change the world?"

"For someone with so many talents, and who is so fond of the riverbank, I would have thought you might show a little more interest!"

"One small boat against a planet full of lemmings?"

"Give us a break! Ease up on all this pathetic small boaty-boat stuff! - I hear that in the eleventh century a certain esquire Flatty of Laleham, was knighted not far from here for his services to his monarch and country."

"It's strange your saying that, for I know of no history books recording such an event," said Flatty.

"Of course..." said the Queen "...if anything so oddly peculiar did still exist from such an age, there would be such a fuss in the papers and on the news that they would not get a moments peace, would they Flatty?"

"I imagine for someone in your position you must know that to be a fact, Ma'am" replied Flatty archly.

"Consider this ..." he continued ; "there is a slight difference between organising a boat trip to Runnymede and saving the planet – don't you think?"

"So I was right!" she said.

"The thing is - Ma'am I don't do planets," said Flatty.

"Don't do? What do you mean 'Don't do'? What exactly are you Flatty? You sound more like an alien from the Planet Zog at times. Not my idea of a rowing boat at all! Take me to your leader – I want a second opinion!"

"Yes ma'am, very funny. But planets are very difficult."

"This conversation is going nowhere!"

"No ma'am."

"And I'm fed up with this 'Yes ma'am, No ma'am, Three bags full of bilge-water flunky stuff. I am most put out! Exceedingly so! Stop it! You hear!"

"Okey Dokey."

"Okey Dokey yourself!"

The two of them paused and looked out to the lake with the sun breaking through.

"Anyway it is in my history book!" she said.

"I did help out in the winter floods," said Flatty.

"I know," she said.

"And at the opening of Parliament," he said.

"I know – I was there, wasn't I!" said the Queen.[2]

"I was thinking," said Flatty "It might be a good idea to flood the Opening of Parliament *every* year. Show a bit of respect for the forces of nature and all that."

"Now you're talking! Both the Ermine Vermin and the Mouldy People could do with a good wash occasionally!" said the Queen.[3]

"And it focuses the mind wonderfully," said Flatty.

"Mind you - that last flood ruined the carpets, and there was stinky mud everywhere. The cleaning bill was horrendous," said the Queen.

"Just a thought ma'am," said Flatty.

"Oh give over! You're back in your flunky voice. Just give me it straight will you?"

"OK The Bokey is the same. Can't stand mud on the carpets."

"Look Flatty, if you want to hide in your jolly willow world, messing about on the river, not taking a wider interest in the world around you – well good luck mate. I'm sure it's all very pleasant. But some people might say you need to grow up and take more responsibility. What about Lucy and Sprinkle? Don't you care what happens to them? Just a thought! Think about it. OK?"

"Yes ma'am. I'll think about it," said Flatty.

"And by the way, technically you are *my* oldest knight" said the Queen.

"Possibly so, if I were technically the same boat" said Flatty.

"Well aren't you?"

"I have had several major refits since then. Hardly a plank of the original left."

"Really?" she said.

"That's right," he said.

"Quite remarkable, but it won't wash... Well Sir Flatty, that bit of you that belongs to me, pay attention!"

---

[2] *Flatty to the Rescue*

[3] *The Queen is referring with some disrespect to the ermine worn by Members of the House of Lords and to Members of Parliament (M.P. for Mouldy Person). She obviously speaking privately to Flatty as a close friend, and could never say such a thing in public. So it might be best if you did not tell anyone else about this.*

"You really want me to flood Parliament every year?" asked Flatty.

"If that's what it takes," she said.

"But people will get hurt," he said.

"No they won't not if you're doing your other job properly, as Official Royal Thames Flood Protection Liaison and Warning Wotnot," replied the Queen.

"That's not right," said Flatty "That's like having a fireman who sets fire to buildings. And what about the cost? Admit it Ma'am - you are off your royal trolley!"

"Now now!" she said "No need to get personal. Was your idea anyway. The question is - can you help things along a bit so that certain people who are a little too set in their ways might become less sure of themselves?"

"By drowning their children?" said Flatty.

"No, You are deliberately being thicker than your construction allows. Nobody needs to drown. We just need to shake folks up a bit. The odd flood will be as nothing compared to the damage of sea level rise. Who could be a better man for the job than yourself, already adapted to living on water?"

"I suppose if everyone lived in boats it might help," said Flatty.

"There you go then - a new idea," said the Queen; "..a fresh insight! Give it some thought, that is all I am asking. OK?"

"Okey Dokey" said Flatty. "Would you like to hear what really happened at the Magna Carta Ma'am?"

"Rather!" said the Queen.

"Are you moored comfortably?"

"Yes. I am quite tied up."

"Then I will begin. In those days there were no locks on the river, to let the boats go up and down past the weirs........."   And so Flatty proceeded to tell the Queen the story of how King John met the rebel Barons at Runnymede and agreed to their demands. This limited the power of the Monarch and ensured the rights of the Barons to fair trial by jury. This agreement, written down and called the Magna Carta, became famous as a foundation stone of democracy. Several copies still exist today. Flatty said he was particularly proud of the part he played in the banning of fish weirs[4]. The story also took a while, because the Queen kept interrupting, especially the bit about Queen Matilda's jewels.[5] So by the time they were finished it was time for tea. Then the Queen gave Lucy and Sprinkle a tour round the dungeons and secret passages – and showed them her jewels - and by the time that was done it was dark. - so they stayed the night.

_____

[4] *Flatty and the Magna Carta.*
[5] *King John had wasted all his money at war with the French, and had to pawn the crown jewels, including his crown, with the Knights Templer. Luckily they let him borrow it back for signing the Magna Carta.*

Shaken not Stirred

Next morning they had boiled eggs and soldiers - with real soldiers. Then it was time to go back through the tunnel, past the grumbling water gate and out onto the river. Simone was still there, discretely watching the floating gin palace.

"Ah Sprinkle. I thought you had gone without saying goodbye."

"Nope!" said Sprinkle "and to prove it, I'm here! Wuff!"

"I was wondering if you wouldn't mind doing me a favour? said Simone. "Lucy says you 'as a good nose, so I wonder if you could go for a little doggy wander, up to the bridge, over the river and back past that boat. Have a sniff around for me, but be very, very discrete. Could you do that?"

"Of course Ma'am!" said Sprinkle "They call me Bond, James Bond. Licensed to kill. British Secret Service at your service."

"Stop it Sprinkle!" said Lucy "And you can take your collar off. It only get's you excited."

"Oh..woof!"

"Sprinkle?!" warned Lucy.

"But it really works!" he said.

"It makes you crazy. You nearly sank Simone when you pulled her rope off the other day. It's messing with your mind – Isn't it Flatty?" said Lucy.

"Ah..." said Flatty, not wanting to be drawn in.

"What do you mean - Ah?" said Lucy " You're meant to be the responsible one!"

Flatty twiddled his oars, thinking.

"He'll be fine!" he said at last "He's a young dog, a bit like a teenager. He wears the collar well." Then turning to Sprinkle he said "Remember when you thought the rope was alive?"

"Yes," said Sprinkle.

"It wasn't really was it?"

"No. Of course not!" said Sprinkle.

"So?"

"So I just got a bit carried away," said Sprinkle.

"Good. Now listen Sprinkle. In a way Lucy is right. The collar can have a funny effect on people – I mean dogs."

"So what should I do?" said Sprinkle.

"It's simple" said Flatty.. "Just remember what Simone asked you, and don't get carried away OK?"

"Okey Bokey!" said Sprinkle.

But Lucy scowled "Well don't blame me if ...

..if he....Does Something!"

Sprinkle crossed the bridge and wandered up the other bank. The collar lay quietly matt and black on his neck. No one was paying any attention on this bright, windy, Saturday morning - full of shoppers and tourists busying themselves along the riverside streets of old Windsor.

He padded past the pastel blue and green hulls of holiday hire boats rafted up together on the visitor moorings, across the concrete apron in front of the rowing club and along to where the French boat was moored.

The air was alive with smells, doggy smells, engine oily smells, painty rope and varnish smells. Here the fresh echoes of this morning's coffee and rolls, and there, in that dark corner, smelt like the back of a pub on a Saturday night. Which is what it was, or had been. Faw! Disgusting! How can they drink that stuff?

"And now! ladies and gentleman! I would like to present an excellent sample of twelve hour old fish and chips, mixed to perfection with a burger and cheese, a kebab, curry and deep fried mars bar – all gently marinated in finest Newcastle Brown with a delicate yellow orange and green brouillard of carrot, peas and sick... Mmmm simply heavenly! But wait, what is this? It can't be? It is! How gross! How disgusting! Brown Windsor Soup! AAAAAH NO!

Whoops! We've arrived. There's the boat! No one about. What have we got? – Onions, garlic, diesel, tobacco – yuck. A half-decent Burgundy, some fish, more fish, almonds, sulphur, burnt wood, and something exotic is happening - I've not met before and... wait for it...yes they just pumped out the toilet! Now that is illegal!! Darn stinking environmental Frenchie terrorist gangsters coming over here and polluting our rivers with their filthy foreign sewage! Well we'll see about that!. Got them!"

An Alsatian on a chain lay half asleep in the boat yard, watching Sprinkle with one eye. "Oh Oh! I've been spotted. Keep cool. Top priority now - get message back to M at HQ and PDQ.

Keep walking, head down. The name's Bond. James Bond.

Do I look like I give a damn? Don't get excited. Self Control. Remember what Flatty said. Ignore him.

...What's that smell?

Ooops! A car is following me!

Perhaps I just better let it pass. Ha ha!

And a good day to you sir! Yes and I'm sure the pedigree of your mother is above reproach too. Do I look like a zombie? Really! Well thank you for asking and I really enjoyed listening to your new car horn. Was it a present? Have a nice day you... you....milk swilling, cat loving.....steady James steady!...."

Sprinkle cautiously averted his eyes and kept his head down, doing his best "I'm minding my own business" act and wagging his tail like the village idiot.

The air was alive with smells, doggy smells

Safe at last, Sprinkle ran down a side street away from the river, doubled back to the bridge and returned to where Flatty and Simone were moored.

"Wuff! We got him. Wuff! We got him!" he called excitedly as he ran up.

"Hush, Sprinkle," said Simone. "What happened?"

"The toilet. They emptied the toilet in the river! We got them. Call the police!"

"What is he saying?" Simone asked Flatty.

"In England you can't empty the toilet in the river. It's illegal" said Flatty.

"Is that it - Sprinkle?"

"Yes I came straight back. Stayed out of trouble. Didn't get excited nor fight no killer dogs nor snaky rope monsters. Mr Ice Man. That's me! We got them haven't we?"

Everyone paused. It was painful.

"You tell him, Simone," said Lucy.

"Tell me what?" said Sprinkle.

"Sprinkle, you did a good job," said Simone. "I am really very pleased you didn't lose your self-control, or raise anybody's suspicions. Good work! But we were looking for real criminal things like guns or drugs."

"But if everyone pollutes the river it will die!" said Sprinkle "Asked Penton. He's always talking about it. It's wrong! They must be stopped!"

"He got a point," said Lucy.

"Sprinkle pe'rraps you 'ave smelt something else too, something important but you do not know eet," said Simone. "Is my fault - I should not 'ave asked you....is a job for a trained dog. But thanks veree much for 'elping."

Poor old Sprinkle! He'd really tried to do it right. Hadn't got into any trouble. Found Johnny Foreigner up to no good, red-handed and what thanks did he get? I bet *she* couldn't tell a Beaujolais from a ...a bacon sandwich!

"Did your collar do anything?" asked Lucy.

"No," said Sprinkle grumpily "Anyway -it doesn't do things. It just makes everything clearer and sharper, unlike *certain people* who do just the opposite!"

"Well there's no need to go into a sulk," said Lucy.

And then it was time to turn round and go home again.

They said their goodbyes to Simone, who still had work to do.

Something the Queen had said in private to Flatty was clearly on his mind, which made him very dull on the way back home. And Sprinkle was fed up – both with letting the smugglers get away and the needless fuss and palaver over the collar. He resolved to become an expert at identifying smells and on the way back down river took every opportunity to rummage through bookshops and libraries for books on the subject.

 Lucy was quiet too. She did not really mind that they had run out of time and not found the source of the Thames. On the way back she humoured Sprinkle, helping him with his smelling tests, but next time - she resolved they would need to plan on a much longer trip, and leave that blasted collar at home!

Something Smells Funny

When they got home Old Boatshed was pleased to see all The Stuff back in its rightful place. All, that is, apart from the collar, which Sprinkle needed for his food and wine tasting evening classes. Police boat Fred brought an inspector down with a suitcase full of samples to test Sprinkle's sense of smell.

"Do you recognise any before I open the bags" said the inspector.

Sprinkle tried them without the collar "Number ten - garlic, fifteen – onions, twenty three.- don't know."

The inspector looked them up in his notebook "Correct, correct and twenty three - that was cocaine - nasty stuff" he announced.

Then Sprinkle tried with the collar on. "One, two, three, four, five, six," announced Sprinkle "seven, eight, nine, ten, eleven twelve thirteen fourteen fifteen sixteen seventeen eighteen nineteen twenty..."

"Stop stop!" said the Inspector "Do you mean you recognise every one?"

"Yep. Amazing ain't it!" said Sprinkle.

"But that list includes every known major drug, plastic explosive, anthrax, gunpowder and ..and Smarties!" said the Inspector in disbelief.

"Nope, definitely not Smarties. I think you'll find their M&Ms – Let me see....this one - bag number seventy one," said Sprinkle.

"Gettaway! You're pulling my leg! Tell me you are joking!" said the Inspector.

"No Straight up! Smarties have more milk solids" said Sprinkle.

"What? ...!!***!" said the Inspector, quite flummoxed.

"Sprinkle, did all these smells come from the boat Simone was watching?"

"Nope."

"Well which ones were from the boat?"

"Garlic, onions, tobacco, fish, almonds, tomatoes, pepper, olives, bread, cheese, Burgundy, beef, salt, pepper, coffee, chocolate, chewing gum, apples-Bramley, orange, onion, wood - er - mahogany, paint, oil - diesel, toilet cleaner of course, rope, ..tributyle tin, ..mm ..nasty, Calvados, epoxy resin, a single malt –and a load of others but mainly fish - but I just can't place the whiskey. Sorry chaps!"

"Fish?" said the Inspector, shaking his head; "whiskey?"

"You might get them on the tributyle tin – Penton says it's illegal" said Sprinkle "You would not believe what it does to dog winkles – outrageous!"[6]

The inspector looked stunned. Who were these crazy people?

"So Inspector - Did you get what you wanted?" asked Lucy with a winning smile.

---

[6] Scientists at the Plymouth Marine Biology Laboratories showed that tri-butyl tin in anti-fouling paint used on boats damaged the fertility of the female Dogwhelk, by causing the growth of a false male organ. Sprinkle may have confused his winkles and whelks - an easy mistake for a young dog to make.

Smells Fishy

Lucy and Sprinkle were fishing in the rain.

"You know that smell?" said Sprinkle.

"Which one?" said Flatty.

"The fishy one, at Windsor," said Sprinkle.

"What about it?" said Flatty.

"T'were fertiliser," said Sprinkle in his best farm boy accent.

"How do you know?" said Flatty.

"When I went to the farm for the papers – some was being delivered."

"You mean the white boat at Windsor?" asked Lucy.

Sprinkle nodded.

"It seems rather odd .. but there's no law against it. If your nose is as sensitive as you claim, maybe they just have had some on board," said Lucy.

"Simone said it eventually went back downstream," said Flatty. "She was following it."

"Did she discover anything?" asked Lucy.

"Just said 'Hello' - couldn't stop, and hoped to see us in France one day."

"What shall we do?" said Lucy.

"I'll tell Police Boat Fred next time I see him," said Flatty "It's probably nothing at all."

"It's funny, aint' it? That's what the fishy smell was. They must put fish in the fertiliser," said Sprinkle, puzzled.

"If you carry on like this my boy, your nose could earn you a lot of money when you grow up," said The Bokey.

"When I'm rich I'm going to buy a trampoline," said Sprinkle.

"Anything else?" asked Lucy. "What if you are very, very rich indeed?"

"I'd buy a bone every day."

"What about other people?" asked Lucy.

"You could have one too if you like," said Sprinkle. "I know. I'd buy the river ..and make it a nature reserve,... ban nasty plastic motor boats, ..buy Penton some new hinges to shut him up... hah! and build a huge riverside doghouse with warm carpets and comfy arm chairs - and have a shed outside where humans could be chained up at night...."

"Sprinkle!" interrupted Lucy crossly "That's most unkind! I never chain you up, and you always sleep on the end of my bed and never in a nasty draughty smelly old dog house!"

"Well you did ask!" he said.

"Well anyway!" said Lucy" If you are so concerned about the river and the little fishes, how come you're fishing?"

"Well anyway yourself!..... I'm a red blooded carnivore ain't I?" said Sprinkle. "James Bond eats fish, and I bet "M" doesn't keep rabbiting on about it."

" No! Its 'Q' in charge and 'M' makes the gadgets."

"No! 'M' is the ...!"

".....Oh put a sock in it, you two. You're scaring the fish away," said Flatty.

Duty Calls

A few days later Charles the Helicopter landed in the back garden and asked Aunty Dolly if he could borrow Flatty and Sprinkle for a meeting in London.

"What for?" she asked.

"Oh nothing much," said Charles "Some flood defence committee work. I was passing by so I thought I'd give them a lift – if they can come..."

"It's all rather inconvenient," said Aunt Dolly, "I was just going into the village for things for tea tonight. Could you come back tomorrow?"

"Actually," said Charles quietly; "It is rather important. Tell you what – give me the shopping list and we'll get your stuff sent round."

"Can I come too?" asked Lucy.

"Sorry," said Charles "Got my orders. You are not invited."

"Humph!" said Sprinkle "If she doesn't go, then I don't go!"

"Nor me," said Flatty.

"Oh lord! A dog with attitude! Whatever next! Just a mo' while I consult my employer.....Hello London. This is Hotel Romeo One - Over ......

....Yes but they won't do it without the girl. .... and by the way – we need a pound of self-raising flour and half a pound of unsalted butter ... delivered to The Bokey this morning or the whole deals off! Got it? Over...

.....Don't worry I'll pay. ....What?   .....No she doesn't want marge......   and half a pound of coley - for the cat - Over and Out!"

Charles turned to Lucy said "Sorry, you can't come in the helicopter – but no one can stop you riding in Flatty. It will be draughty so put these flying togs on. The helmets have radio mikes so we can talk. When you're ready we'll pick up Flatty and whiz up to town."

"Wow! Is that cool or what?" said Sprinkle.

"If it isn't now it will be by the time you get to London, so wrap up well – and try not to fall out!" said Charles.

Charles made Lucy put on one of his spare flying suites. It was far too big and did nothing for her looks. But Charles insisted, so on it went, with a flying helmet and goggles. Sprinkle said it made her look like a cross between an astronaut and a slinky toy. Then it was Sprinkles turn, but only the goggles would fit, so Lucy wrapped a long woolly scarf around him. Then Lucy tied them both to Flatty, to stop them falling out.

When Charles was satisfied he took off, hovered in the middle of the river and lowered two stout loops of webbing into the water, which Flatty rowed into - so there was one under the bows, and one under the stern. Then Charles opened the throttle and rose up, lifting them dripping high above the great willow trees, and swung round to follow the river downstream to London.

"Welcome aboard flight Romeo One bound for London," said Charles.

"We will be flying at a height of three hundred feet. The weather today in London is calm and sunny. Your flight attendant, Lucy, will be around shortly with a light snack and drinks after demonstrating the use of lifejackets and the emergency exit procedure."

"You gotta be joking!" yelled Lucy
"Sit down Sprinkle or you'll fall out!"
"Wow!" said Sprinkle "Wuff wuff, wow, bow wow wuff fantastic!
Don't you just love it?
Howooooo!.......Ruff ruff ruff!"

Battersea

Sprinkle was learning rapidly that things were not always as they seemed. The cooling-water intake from the river up to Battersea Power Station was no exception. Just inside the tunnel, under the footpath, was a hidden boat lock.

Normally both sides of the lock were open, for maintenance boats to service the cooling-water intake, and you went straight through under the towpath and along a short channel. But today both gates swung shut, closing off the sunlight and river sounds.

Somewhere a machine started, and the water level began to drop.

"But there is no downstream!" said Lucy. We have just come in from the river.

Everything flows into the river and down to the sea, so we can't go down!"

"Looks like we are," said Flatty. "Charles said to just keep going and we'd get there."

Wet slimey stone walls rose dripping above them as they sank deeper and deeper underground.

"I'm glad you have your collar on Sprinkle!" said Lucy with a shiver.

In the light fromf Sprinkle's collar a large gate slid into view.

The water level stopped falling, and the gate opened
to reveal an illuminated tunnel.

"Right troops, forwards on both engines,"
said Flatty and he set off down the tunnel,
which curved away into the distance.

After a while Flatty said; "We must be close to Vauxhall bridge"
"Glad someone knows," said Lucy. "It's all as clear as mud to me."
A gate opened to reveal a harbour, humming with activity.
"Welcome Flatty - Please Dock at Gate Number Three," boomed a voice
over a loudspeaker. Rows of green lights lit up, like landing lights,
beckoning them on into a covered dock.

Inside was laid out like a conference room, around a huge central table. At one end were places for boats, and at the other end there were seats for people to sit.

"Hi Flatty!" called a rubber inflatable boat. It was Windy. "Glad you could make it. And this must be Sprinkle. How do you do? We have heard a lot about you. ...And Lucy. Hello I'm Winderemere, Special Boat Squadron."

"Hello," said Lucy "If you don't mind my saying, it's a most peculiar set up for a flood defence committee."

"Ah," said Windy looking puzzled; "So no one has explained....?"

"Nope!" said Flatty, Sprinkle and Lucy together.

"Well, OK. I don't know how much Flatty told you about the Opening of Parliament , but he was a bit of a hero and ever since we have been keeping an eye on him."

"You mean you've been spying on us?" said Lucy.

"No, no not at all! But Flatty and Sprinkle might ....could...er.... help out with something."

"And that is?" said Lucy.

"The Olympics!" said Windy. " Big security headache. Everyone is involved. VIPs visiting, large crowds, terrorist threats. You name it and we are planning for it. Big op! You wouldn't believe the paperwork... well anyway - the thing is the Chinese are bringing the Olympic torch over by boat, and we,, er wondered ..."

"You want Sprinkle and Flatty to help?" said Lucy.

"....Eeee....a yes!" said Windy.

"And protect everyone from terrorists bombs?" said Lucy.

"Well, I was thinking more diplomatic liaison kind of work," said Windy.

"Uh huh! My thoughts entirely," said Sprinkle nodding. "I'm very good with people."

"So what, exactly...?" said Flatty.

"We want you to escort the Chinese from international waters, up the Thames to Greenwich, and see the Olympic Flame safely ashore," said Windy.

"Wow! Bow! Bow Wow! Wow in the bow!" said Sprinkle.

"I think that's a yes," said Flatty with a smile.

"Oh no it's not!" said Lucy "I'm the mummy, and Sprinkle is only young, and you can't go round shoving the nation's youth into danger just like that!"

"You are right of course," said Windy gently; "and it's not for me to say. But there are certain diplomatic sensitivities with the Chinese. For instance, they might not want their battleships to be escorted up the Thames by our battleships, or even be directed by a Port of London pilot. It is a matter of national pride or what they call "face". At the same time we obviously don't want the Chinese navy - fully armed with bullets up their spouts, as it were - in the middle of London – if you get my drift."

"So what do I care?" said Lucy crossly.

"Whereas Flatty here is seen as a more neutral figure," Windy continued. "And Sprinkle here, with his collar on, can find our far more about what is in the Chinese warships than the whole of MI5. Ain't that so Sprinkle?"

"Wuff" said Sprinkle in agreement, with a steely glint eastwards in his eyes.

"Hold your horses! Not so fast. Sprinkle is not an unbiased neutral observer in all this are you Sprinkle?" said Lucy.

"Am too!" said Sprinkle.

"So what about when Auntie Dolly said the Chinese eat dogs? ..Eh? You went bonkers didn't you!"

"Is this true Sprinkle?" asked Windy.

"How would you like it if you were sent somewhere full of cannonballs what eat boats?" said Sprinkle; "T'aint hardly surprising is it?"

"Hm I'd guess I'd be on my guard," said Windy.

"Don't worry about it chaps," said Flatty. "He's with me".

"What you all seem to be forgetting is that the problem is not with Her Majesties' Government. The problem is with me! The problem is 'I say No!" said Lucy.

"Ah!" said Windy. "I guess you'll have to do it on your own Flatty."

"Perhaps Lucy could come along, if she's willing?" said Flatty.

For once Lucy had nothing to say.

At that point a door opened and a woman entered, smartly dressed in a dark grey knee-length skirt and a tailored jacket. She walked briskly over.

"Good morning Lucy, Sprinkle, Flatty," she said. "Welcome to MI5. Call me 'M'. Sorry I could not meet you earlier. You know Lucy – you are absolutely right - it just would not work if Flatty and Sprinkle were to greet and escort the Olympic flame."

"Why's that?" said Lucy.

"Can you imagine the Chinese handing over the sacred flame to a dog in a boat? They'd have a fit. And the world's press would turn it into a complete joke! Whichever way you look at it - it would be a disaster."

"So what do you want?" said Lucy.

"We need you, Lucy. It must be you that greets the Chinese. You will represent the flower of youth, of future generations. You are a very pretty child..... well, perhaps with a bit of a wash! Children are highly revered in China. You will be the Olympic welcoming committee. What could be more wholesome than a young girl with her puppy in a simple rowing boat?"

"Puppy!" snorted Sprinkle outraged.

"A bit of a wash?" snorted Lucy.

"Simple?" said Flatty.

"I think a boy would be better than a girl, don't you Flatty?" said Windy.

"What? What boy?" asked Lucy.

"I disagree, of course. I have always felt that women can do most jobs at least as well as men, if not better. Don't you agree Lucy?" said M.

"Absolutely!" said Lucy indignantly "Of course girls are better!

"That's right," said M "We need someone to greet them, lead them up the Thames and transfer them from the anchorage to the shore. It will be quite safe on the water. If there is to be any trouble it is much more likely to on land where the crowds are. How about it Lucy? I need your help. Britain and the Olympics need you. Will you do it?"

"Oh all right then. I suppose someone's got to do it. And we can't let a boy make a mess of it!" said Lucy.

Sprinkle's collar... one, MI5...zero

"Flatty Can Q, our Chief Engineer, study your collar," asked Windy.

"It will only work if Sprinkle wears it," said Flatty.

"Let's look at the collar on its own first," said Q. "That's more scientific."

"I'd be careful with that thing if I were you," said Flatty.

"Poof! We are looking at gadgets all the time. There's nothing under the sun we haven't had to deal with here, one time or another." said Q.

Half an hour later Q came back with the collar, looking rather glum.

"We got zilch, nothing. It's like an inert lump of ..inert lumpy stuff. Not a dicky bird!

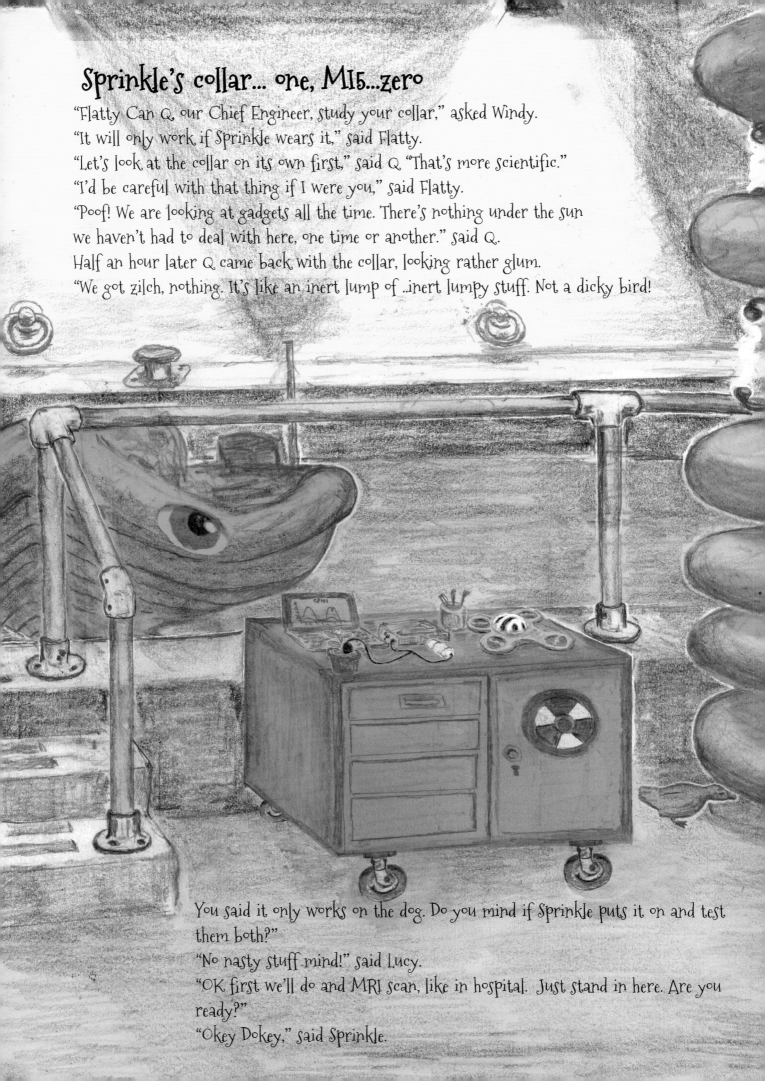

You said it only works on the dog. Do you mind if Sprinkle puts it on and test them both?"

"No nasty stuff mind!" said Lucy.

"OK first we'll do and MRI scan, like in hospital. Just stand in here. Are you ready?"

"Okey Dokey," said Sprinkle.

"Stay as still as possible" said Q.
He pressed a button and the machine started to hum, and vibrate, ..and rattle... and the noise grew louder and louder...

A green haze was shimmering around Sprinkle's collar, and he began grinning manically.
"Turn it off!" shouted Flatty above the roar.

Electricity flickered out from the collar and sizzled around the rim of the doughnut.
The noise and vibration grew louder.
The air crackled with green static.
Lucy's hair stood on end.

With loud bang and a blinding flash Lucy found herself suddenly dazzled,
deafened,
and in the dark.

Klaxons started to alarm, the emergency lights came on, and overhead sprinklers drenched everyone.

Soldiers and fire fighters rushed into the room looking startled.
The scanner lay in piece on the floor, smoking and sizzling with electricity.

As her sight returned and the ringing in her ears faded, Lucy found
Sprinkle sitting happily, lit by the glow of his collar.
"Wow!" said Sprinkle "That was great! What a charge!
Can we do it again?"

"Oh blimey," said Q "It's ruined. That cost
two million!"
"Did I not say be careful!" said Lucy "I am
not at all pleased that you placed my dog in a
machine which blew itself up. You deliberately
put him at risk! It is not good enough!
Until I am convinced you know what
you are doing, I will not permit you
to experiment any further!
Good day to you sir!
Come on gang, we are out of here!"

It's not quite ready yet, is it?" said Flatty
to Q as they left.

"Q - I want to see you in my office
NOW!" said M as she stormed out.

"Oh Lord!" said Q surveying the mess.

The Olympic Torch arrives

Flatty, Lucy and Sprinkle were waiting out to sea near the mouth of the Thames.

The first to arrive was a large Chinese battleship.

"Welcome to Britain!" called Flatty in very formal and correct Chinese when it was within hailing distance.

The great ship slowed to a stop. Compared to Flatty it was huge.

"Where is the Olympic Welcoming Committee?" it boomed out.

"That's us," said Flatty.

"In the name of the British Olympic Committee we welcome the Olympic Torch Bearer to Great Britain and thank you for delivering the Olympic flame to our shores.

If the honoured Torch Bearer would like to step aboard we will proceed up river. For your part in accompanying the torch we thank you and we welcome the Chinese Navy as honoured guests."

"But little boat, I cannot hand the great Olympic Torch over to you. You are too small and it would be disrespectful to our country and the great Olympic tradition", said the Battleship.

"I assure you that it would be no disrespect to put the Torch in our company," said Flatty.

"What is the matter?" asked Lucy. "What are you saying Flatty?"

"The battleship is concerned that we are not important enough to receive the Torch," said Flatty.

"Tell him about the time you were in China," said Sprinkle.

"Perhaps you are right, But I hate pulling rank," said Flatty. "Oh well, here goes" and he spoke to the battleship in Chinese again.

"Where I come from we are accustomed to paying respect to our ancestors, our great family lines and our Emperors," said Flatty.

"We too revere the great leaders and families of the past" said the battleship.

"So I am disappointed that the chop of the Great Emperor Yu is not treated with the respect it deserves," said Flatty.

"What is this? What do you mean?" said the battleship startled.

"There was a time when the Emperor would have sunk any vessel that ignored his personal seal," said Flatty, using the Chinese form of address from a superior to his inferior.

"But the Emperor Yu has been dead for 3000 years!" replied the battleship.

"Would you agree that his legacy lives on?" asked Flatty.

"Of course, every good Chinese learns of Emperor Yu's great deeds taming China's Sorrow, and the Great River. But why do you speak of these things?"

"Look closely at my bow, my friend and tell me what you see," said Flatty softly.

The battleship came closer, and closer.

"Look out, it's going to run us over!" said Lucy.

"No it's OK. He's just taking a look at the seal on my bows," said Flatty.

"What seal?" said Lucy.

"An emperor gave it me a long time ago. It shows that I am the head of the Chinese navy. Let's see how the battleship reacts," said Flatty.

"Where did you get that?" said the Battleship, startled.

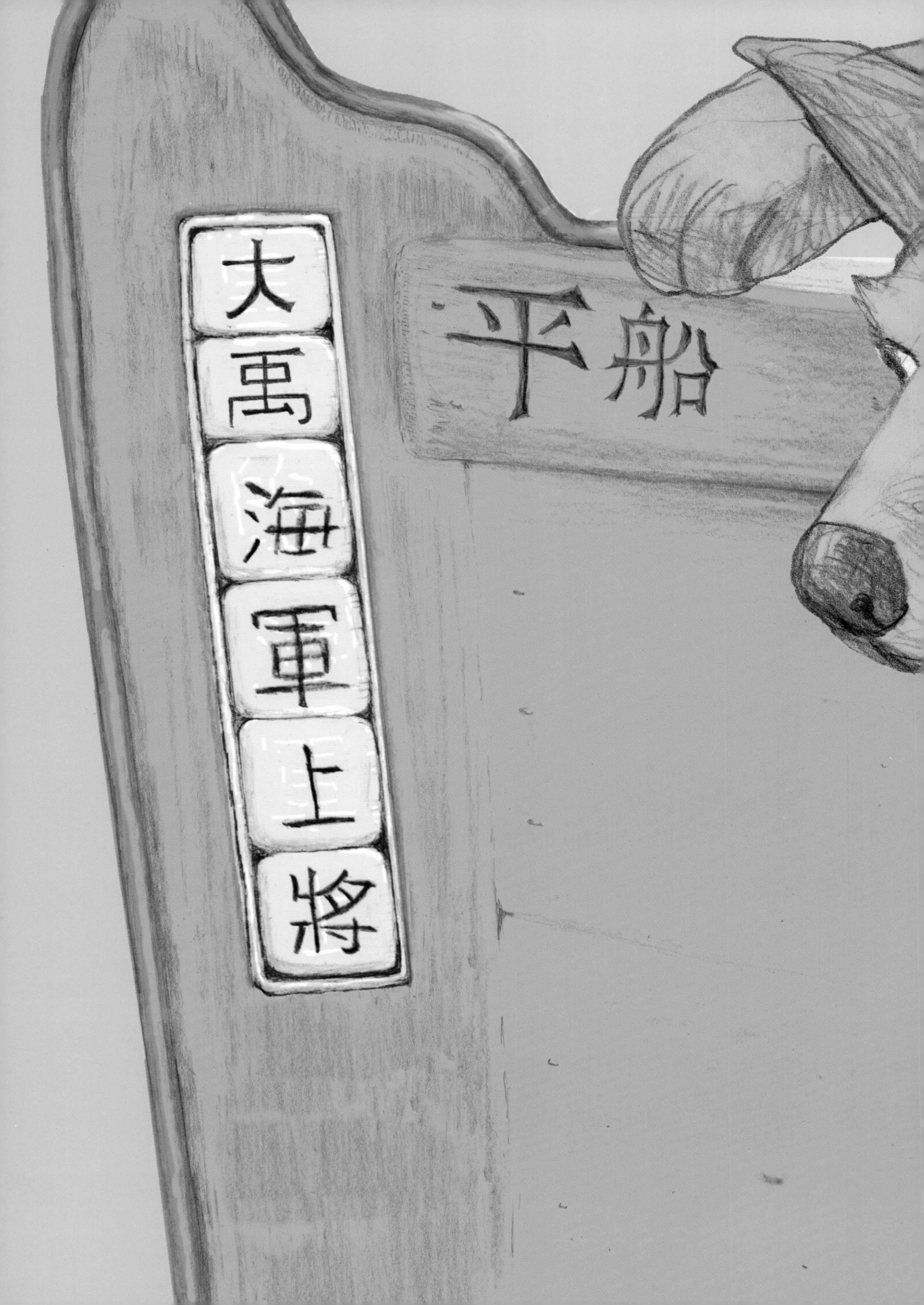
大禹海軍上將
平船

"It is not working out very well," said Flatty. "I should not have tried to lord it over them. The politicians in Beijing will not want to hand over the flame when they find out who I am. I should have thought this through more carefully."

The battleship had sharp ears and was listening.
He surprised Flatty by speaking in perfect English.
"If you are who you say you are, it would cause a sensation in China. Don't quote me, old chap, but there is quite a lot of internal unrest in our country at the moment. The last thing our government wants is someone like yourself to crawl out of the woodwork and unite a load of ungrateful trouble makers."
"You sound to me as if you are already half-persuaded," said Flatty.
"I'm admitting nothing," said the battleship. "But a good officer should be prepared for anything, and ..er...well I pride myself in my ear for local dialects. Quite frankly your accent and form of address is not so much foreign as very ancient.
Some of the words you use are old fashioned too. I can't believe your secret service capable of training a spy to speak in such a way."

"And why would Her Majesties Government invest so much effort in teaching me to speak in the ancient Chinese way just to escort the Olympic Torch ashore?

If they were capable of such things surely they would reserve it for something of greater consequence," said Flatty.

"Perhaps the West wishes to use the Olympics to ferment revolution in China. It would not be the first time," said the battleship.

"Can we go now?" said Lucy." I'm bored and need a wee."

Just then Lucy's mobile rang. "It's the PM. Says the Olympic Committee have asked him if everything is OK?."

"Tell him they are not ready to hand over the Olympic Flame yet — they need to check my identity," said Flatty.

"Hello, No I'm sorry Mr PM - the Chinese doesn't think Flatty is important enough to hand over to," said Lucy "...........I'm very sorry. ....Yes I know the whole world is watching. ....We didn't say anything nasty or rude - honest!.........................I'll put him on. Hold on please.

Flatty — The PM wants to talk to you."

"Hello PM," said Flatty "They're checking with Beijing................I don't know how long..........It might take several days..........................Ok I'll ask - hang on."

Flatty turned to the battleship and speaking in formal Chinese again said "Our Prime Minister respectfully suggests that the Olympic and Chinese traditions of celebrating and inspiring our children is a worthy ideal. Indeed our Olympic Committee planned it this way all along. He respectfully asks how long this delay might take and says, if it would help matters, you could hand over to someone else if you like. We are happy to consider any solution that is agreeable. Would you prefer to hand over to our largest aircraft carrier?"

"That may not be necessary. Just a moment while I talk to Beijing," said the Chinese battleship. "Please convey our respects to you honoured Prime Minister. His interesting suggestion is being studied carefully. I am sure we can find a solution which is acceptable to everyone. Forgive me if I cannot reply immediately, in China it is night time."

"The PM asks what he is saying," said Lucy.

"They are all in bed. It may take a little while," said Flatty.

A television channel helicopter flew over. Images of a small rowing boat facing the battleship started to appear on the world news.

The PM rang Lucy again "The press are on our backs wanting to know what the delay is about. They are presenting it as a confrontation between you and the Chinese navy. This is not the image we want to present. The Olympics is about friendship and goodwill between nations."

"But I need to go to the loo!" Lucy replied.

 "Perhaps she could come on board, prior to the transfer ceremony, to greet the Torch Bearer?" said Flatty to the battleship.

"Of course," said the battleship. "I will immediately invite both parties aboard for refreshments."

"Well done!" said the PM "My Press Office will announce that immediately, and perhaps the battleship will allow the press helicopter come close to take picture?"

"Good idea," said the battleship. "I will even invite them to land to record the historic event. That will buy us a couple of hours at least"

Finally a film crew appeared on the the deck of the battleship, and when all was ready it spoke again; "Honoured Admiral Flatty I salute you and offer my apologies for the short delay as we ..ere.. wait for the tide, to take the Olympic Flame up your famous Thames river. Your presence at this ceremony is a great honour for the Chinese People and links our two great nations together through the venerable history of our great waterways, irrigation systems and flood defences - built by China's greatest engineer and leader – Emperor Yu. My government is deeply honoured that our Olympic sailing ship may follow you into London and in the sprit of international friendship and good will I respectfully request permission to escort you safely into London."

"Okey Dokey – I'll ask," said Flatty "Lucy - tell the PM we are on our way and say the battleship wants to come too. Is that OK?"

"The PM asks the battleship to give his word he will not arm his guns whilst a guest in our waters," said Lucy after talking to the PM.

"What do you reckon then?" Flatty asked the battleship.

"I give my word," said the battleship.

The procession set off. Flatty lead with Lucy carrying the Olympic Torch. Next came a traditional Chinese sailing junk followed by the battleship, both carrying streams of flags and banners along decks and masts.

As they neared the Thames Barrier Sprinkle started to look agitated.

"What's the matter Sprinkle?" said Lucy.

"There's that smell again, fertiliser, really strong!" he said.

"But we are miles from the coast. Surely you can't smell that far?" said Flatty.

"It's that barge!" said Sprinkle.

An old dumpy Thames rubbish barge was slowly making it's way out to sea.

"It is just a stinky rubbish barge," said Flatty "He goes out every day and dumps the rubbish in deep water."

"No, it's a bomb!" said Sprinkle.

Stop Barging In!

"Don't be silly," said Lucy. "It can't be a bomb. How do you know?"

"It's a fertiliser bomb. I smelled one when that customs officer gave me those smelling tests. Don't you remember?" said Sprinkle.

"Why would anyone want to?.....Oh Golly....you don't think. He's not aiming for us is he?"

"In five minutes time both he and us will be going through the Thames Barrage," said Flatty "... watched by the world's press. What a perfect opportunity, to wreck the Olympic Games - and flood London - and create an international incident with China." "We have to stop him. Lucy, get the PM, quick...............Not available? ...It's Flatty here and its urgent.....well knock on the door!.....thank you! Yes I'm sorry to interrupt...You're washing your hands—right.. now the thing is we think there's a bomb on the Thames barge. Sprinkle smelt it.........Yes but he's never been wrong!   You heard what happened at MI5?   So...Can you stop it? .... Well - sink it or blow it up before it reaches us
...................Five minutes, no longer.   Ok I'll wait"

8

"These things take time. You just can't go round blowing up things. There are people on board the barge. What if Sprinkle were wrong? That's what the PM said," said Flatty.

"What does he say?" asked Sprinkle.

"I say there!" said Flatty to the battleship. We think there's a bomb on that barge. Please stand off, and keep away from it OK?"

"Of course," said the battleship and with a whooping warning klaxon he changed direction taking the Chinese junk and Torch Bearer with him.

"But the Thames Barrage!" said Lucy.
The phone rang. "The PM says they are not going to blow up a barge and kill people on the word of a dog!" said Lucy. "He says to stay away from it and you'll be fine."

"Put him on....." said Flatty ".... Ok I'll see what I can do".
....The PM can't help!"

Networking

Flatty raced over the waves towards one of the huge buoys marking the shipping lane.

"Got that rope ready?" called Flatty.

"Ready!" called Lucy.

"Let go!" said Flatty and Lucy dropped a plastic float, as big as a football, over the side with the rope attached.

As Flatty circled the huge shipping-lane buoy Lucy paid out the rope until they returned to the float.

"Tie her off good and tight now," said Flatty. "Quickly, the barge is nearly here."

"Ready!" called Lucy. The end of the rope was now tied to the shipping lane buoy.

Whilst Flatty took them racing across the bows of the oncoming barge, Lucy and Sprinkle paid out the rope.

They were now almost directly in front of it.

"Stop!" called Lucy "Quick, Sprinkle, give me the end of the net!"

"I can't find it!" said Sprinkle, rummaging around under a huge mound of fishing net.

"Quickly Sprinkle!" called Lucy.

"Hurry – it's coming!" called Flatty.

At last Sprinkle found the end of the net, tied it to the rope, and chucked it over the side.

"Be careful – mind your legs - don't get tangled up," said Flatty and he started again, crossing in front of the barge as Lucy and Sprinkle paid out the rest of the net.

"You're never going to catch this fish," called Sprinkle finally all the net was out.

"Hang on - Don't let go yet. We want the barge to ride well over the top," called Flatty.

They waited.

Now the front of the barge was crossing over the sunken net.

It was half way over.

"Go for it Flatty!" called Lucy, and Flatty started away from the barge as fast as possible, pulling the net tight up underneath it.

"Let go!" called Flatty.

The barge was nearly past.

"Can't. It is stuck!" called Lucy.

Suddenly Flatty was being dragged backward through the water, closer and closer towards the giant half-submerged propeller blade chopping the sea at the back of the barge, which was wrapping the net around and around.

"Cut the rope!" he called.

"I can't!" called Lucy.

"Sprinkle!" called Flatty.

They were being dragged under the propeller!

Sprinkle leapt on the rope and bit it, and bit it. His collar glowered red.
The rope was parting but there wasn't enough time!
Desperately Lucy seized the old wooden paddle. She raised it high above her head, like
some great medieval battle axe.

Her arms felt hot and hugely powerful - adrenaline coursed her body like electricity. With a terrifying scream she let go every reserve, every control, save her focus on the rope.

Down came the blade, transformed beyond physics, cleaving the air with unstoppable force. The cable was cut, but the sword had not finished its journey yet, narrowly missing Sprinkle's neck, it ended up deep in Flatty's woodwork.

Twang! the rope parted. They all flinched and fell back in the boat

"Time to go," said Flatty and he shot away from the barge as fast as he could go.

"Is it going to work?" asked Lucy.

"There!" said Sprinkle.

The huge shipping lane buoy was being dragged towards the back of the barge. It hit the side of the ship and was dragged under. With a fearful crash and the shrieking of torn metal, the propeller, the buoy and its mooring chain became a tangle of twisted steel wrapped and grinding together.
The barge was now firmly attached to the giant mooring chain of the shipping lane buoy, anchored on the sea bed.
Then its propeller shaft fractured, the engines started to race, and smoke poured out of the smoke stack. But the barge was going nowhere. It slowed to a halt, anchored firmly to the bottom..

"I have got a bad feeling about this" said Sprinkle.

"Time to retire to a safe distance," said Flatty and they sped further away.

"And what do you think you're playing at?" demanded the Thames Barrier.
The phone rang. It was the PM. "I say Flatty. Steady on! What do you think....."

"BOOOM!"

The PMs voice was drowned by the sound of the barge exploding.
A deafening blast swept over the sea, followed by a small tidal wave.
Debris, fish and water rained out of the sky.
Fire and smoke rose hundreds of feet into the air.

Lucy and Sprinkle stayed low in Flatty waiting for the shock to pass.
As the noise and the smoke cleared Sprinkle looked out towards the barge.
Nothing remained.
Both the barge and the shipping lane buoy were gone.

Sprinkle sniffed dismissively, then remembered the phone "Anything else we can do for you PM?" he asked.

"Gor Blimey! Is everyone OK?" came the PM's voice.

"Here give it to me!" said Lucy "PM - This is Lucy. I am very annoyed! How dare you put Sprinkle and Flatty and me in such danger! Whilst you skulk around hiding in your bunker! It's not good enough. If I were a grown up I'd...."

"....Easy up shipmate!" said Flatty. "Let me talk to the PM."

Scowling Lucy handed the phone back to Flatty.
"Sorry about that PM," he said. "The blast was quite unsettling."

"No she's right," said the PM. "We were too concerned about not upsetting the Chinese. I shouldn't have let it happen."

"Anyway, the good news is the coast is clear," said Flatty "So we can press on up river to London."

"Well done, all of you. See you later," said the PM, ringing off.

The Chinese warship joined Flatty again. "Your security arrangements are most imaginative," it said.

"Thank you for your generous assistance," said Flatty "I'm sorry but we appear to have slightly damaged your net."

"Think of it as our contribution to the celebrations. I do like things to go with a bang. Should you require any further assistance clearing a safe passage up the Thames - we still have a little netting left!.......and perhaps I could send over my surgeon over to sew up your dog?"

Lucy looked at Sprinkle. His shoulder was covered in blood and half an ear was missing. It was her fault. She had lost control. For a moment, wielding that oar, she had felt so powerful, so comfortable, a power and a madness had possessed her, everything she despised was there, deep in her dark soul, exposed in a flash. She had nearly murdered him! What kind of monster was she really? She burst into tears and hugged him " Oh Sprinkle, I'm so sorry - I don't know what came over me?" she cried.

"Now you come to mention it, it does hurt a little - but wasn't that fantastic!" said Sprinkle "Quite the best fun I've had for ages!"

"There appears to be more to that oar than meets the eye," said the battleship.

Indeed, the wooden blade of the oar had clean broken away, revealing a shining burnished silver steel sword blade.

"I thought I felt something tickle," said Flatty. "Luckily we have not sprung a leak, but if you bleed any more Sprinkle you'll ruin the paintwork - and sink us anyway! So let's get this mess cleared up shipmates. The whole world is waiting and we have an Olympic Torch to deliver!"

Nearly THE
END

Wait for it......

THE END

Hope you enjoyed Flatty's adventure.

The author as a young man (on the right)

Here are some important announcements...

No boats, fish or worms were injured writing this book.

On recycled compost
by recycled compost
for recycled compost.

Excessive use of stories can cause unpleasant things to happen and may result in a failure to maintain due care and attention when entering locks, and cause riverbank erosion if travelling at high speeds in excess of three knots.
YOU HAVE BEEN WARNED ☹

A generous helping of Flatty can provide up to 40% of the recommended daily amount (RDA) for a well-balanced narrative and an appreciation of the importance of the riverbank. ☺

The information contained in this book has been obtained by **Inter-Galactic Composting™** from sources believed to be reliable. However, because of the possibility of human, nematode, piscatorial and/or aquatic errors by our sources, Inter-Galactic Composting, or others, Inter-Galactic Composting, its associates, relatives, friends and pets do not guarantee the accuracy, adequacy, suitability for epistemological inference, educational value, or completeness of any information, anywhere, ever, and particular not today, and are not responsible for any errors or omissions, natural disasters, social unrest or wet floor-boards which could, may or may not result from the use of such information, but it can help if you carry a sponge and bailer with you at all times.